# THE SNAIL PATROL

When George McDuff's garden is overrun by snails there seems no hope for his cabbage patch. Enter Darren Winterburn, businessman and boy next door. Armed with torch, jamjar and a pocketful of spinach, Darren's mission is to rid the garden of snails from the dinkiest Tiny Whorler to the mightiest Cabbage Buster! But when Mr McDuff refuses to pay for Darren's services, a snail beyond his wildest imaginings slithers along to exact revenge. It's big, it's slimy and what's more it talks! Stand by for a close encounter of the gastropodic kind. Get ready for *The Snail Patrol*.

This hilarious, anarchic book, is wonderfully illustrated by Philip Reeve, himself a prize-winning author.

# Other books by Chris d'Lacey

FLY, CHEROKEE, FLY – Transworld

FIRE WITHIN – Orchard Books

SALT PIRATES OF SKEGNESS – Orchard Books

RIVERSIDE UNITED! – Transworld

CHRIS D'LACEY

# THE
# SNAIL
# PATROL

*Illustrated by Philip Reeve*

BARN OWL BOOKS

Originally published in 1998 by Scholastic Ltd
This edition first published 2003 by Barn Owl Books
157 Fortis Green Road, London N10 3LX
Barn Owl Books are distributed by Frances Lincoln
4 Torriano Mews, Torriano Avenue, London NW5 2RZ

Text copyright © 1998, 2003 Chris Lacey
Illustrations copyright © 1998, 2003 Philip Reeve
ISBN 1-903015-30-8

Designed and typeset by Douglas Martin Associates
Printed and bound in Great Britain by
Creative Print and Design Wales, Ebbw Vale

# CHAPTER ONE

This is Helix aspersa . . . commonly known as the garden snail. It is a small, gentle, slow-moving creature that slithers about on one large foot. It can stick like glue to any vertical surface and climb a garden wall in about . . . a day. Its favourite food is fresh green cabbages.

Like the cabbages you'd find in
this garden here . . .

This garden belongs to Mr George McDuff. He is a large, bad-tempered, reasonably quick-moving creature that lives at No.2, Poddledown Crescent. He gets around on size twelve feet and is often to be found with his nose squashed flat against his patio doors, looking for signs of *Helix* in his garden. If he sees one, *he* can go up the garden wall in less than a second. George, like the snails, is very fond of cabbages. He has tried everything he knows to keep the snails off his cabbage patch. Here are just a few examples . . .

[1] crushing them underfoot – but this is a messy, slippery business that once gave rise to a twisted ankle, four days in bed, and an army of snails on the garden lawn . . .

[2] setting beer traps - an old granny's trick, which has never been known to capture a snail, but no doubt explains the wavy trails they leave on the patio . . .

[3] firing stones at them from a catapult – a tricky and somewhat destructive procedure, as the ricochet from shells of particularly tough snails can often carry stones through greenhouse windows . . .

[4] dressing up like a giant cabbage — an ancient mystic ruse designed to lure the snails away from the real thing. Unfortunately, most snails just fall about laughing . . .

[5] building the Helix ejector pad — a cunning device triggered by the weight of the snails themselves.

Excellent at shooting unsuspecting snails into hanging baskets, window boxes and, as luck would have it one afternoon, on to the head of the boy next door . . .

This is Darren Winterburn. he lives at No. 4 Poddledown Crescent. He is a scruffy, but deceptively sharp-witted creature that likes playing football, collecting conkers, riding his bike and digging wax out of his ears – though not all at the same time, naturally. His favourite food is fish and chips with lashings of yummy tomato sauce – and he absolutely, positively does *not* like CABBAGES.

But it is surprising what a clonk on the head can do . . .

When the snail bounced off Darren's bonce his first thought was this:

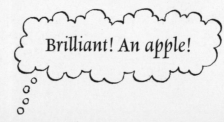

*Brilliant! An apple!*

He snatched it up straight away from the ground and was preparing to take an apple-sized bite – when the snail came slithering out of its shell.

"Ugh," went Darren, closing his mouth, "you're not an apple! Where did you come from?"

It was like a miracle. The snail yawned once, then wound its way fully out of the shell and looked back over Darren's shoulder. Darren followed the snail's gaze. This is what he saw above the garden wall . . .

SNAILS GO HOME

The placard floated off behind a tree. It reappeared a few seconds later, travelling in the opposite direction and bearing the message: **No More Snails!** Mystified, Darren climbed on to the garden bench and peeked, cautiously, over the wall. There was his neighbour, Mr McDuff, holding the placard tight to his shoulder and pacing up and down his garden path. He was muttering things in that growly sort of Scottish than Darren could never quite understand (it sounded like the noise Mark Webberley's dog made when it was lying in front of the fire-place, dreaming). At first, Darren merely shrugged. Mr McDuff was as barmy as a teacake and the Winterburns never had much to do with him. But the messages on the placard niggled Darren's brain:

Darren glanced at the snail that had bounced off his head. It was slithering along the palm of his hand, trying to reach a nearby clematis plant. Darren scratched his ear and frowned in thought. He stuck out his tongue and touched his nose. This only ever happened when he was about to have one of his unfathomably brilliant MONEY-MAKING ideas. Darren had a LOT of money-making ideas. And this time, he was working up a real CRACKER. It took the form of a simple equation:

£ £ £ £ £ £
£ McDuff – Snails = Possible Pots of Dosh £
£ £ £ £ £

That night, after tea, Darren sat on his bed with his knees pulled up underneath his chin – and had a good think . . .

he thought about George . . .
he thought about the snails . . .
but he thought most of all
about his "wanted" list . . .

Darren's list of things to buy
when Mega-rich...
A pair of trainurs with a tick on
the side
A purple bike hat
A giant bar of ~~Tobalurr~~ ~~Tobularon~~ Chocolut
A CD by the Solar Flares — ace!
A komputer game (Robotroids of
Gobbuldygook 7)
A footy shirt with the names of ALL
the Man United Playurs on it
(reserves as well)

When PING! Suddenly, it came to
him. The simplest money-making
scheme EVER! He dashed to his desk
for a sheet of paper and a box of
coloured pencils. Then he sat himself
down and wrote out a leaflet.

It went like this . . .

HAVING TRUBBLE WITH THESE→ 🐌 ?
Let the **SNAIL PATROL** Remuve them from
Your gardun

TINY WORLERS -10p     PUPPY DOG TAILS - 20p

CREAM TOPPERS -30p   CATHERINE WHEEULS-40p

CABBAGE BUSTERS-50p

DISPOSAL CARRIED OUT EFFISHUNTLY AND
HUMAINLY.

PLEASE REPLY TO DARREN, No 4  POODLE DOWN CRESCENT

That evening, Darren posted the
leaflet through Mr McDuff's door. Lo
and behold, as he went to bring in the
milk the next morning, he found a
badly-scrawled note sticking out of the
letterbox . . .

Dear Darren
I am at my WIT's END! Dont DELAY!
Come NOW! Come this INSTANT! Come
YESTERDAY if you can! Just COME!
Mr McDuff (George)

Darren read the note and howled like
a wolf.

The Snail Patrol was in business!

## CHAPTER TWO

Now it just so happened that at the very moment Darren was letting off his wolf impression, a strange little man called Albert Bunker was twiddling the settings on his wide-range, early-warning snowfall detector.

Albert Bunker is a great inventor. He is the man who invented corduroy socks, spaghetti-flavoured pop and the dand-ruff hoover. His snowfall detector was a work of genius. If it heard the sound of snowflakes falling anywhere within a ten-mile radius, it immediately erected a giant umbrella over the entire Bunker residence. Unfortunately, if it heard the sound of a howling wolf it simply exploded and toppled off the roof . . .

"Wolves!" exclaimed Albert, snatching his headphones off. "There are howling wolves in the district, Sharon!" Sharon was Albert's eleven-year-old daughter. She had red hair and freckles. She was in Darren's class.

"I bet it's Darren," Sharon sighed. "He always howls when he's feeling happy."

Albert came over and tousled her hair. "He could be feeling lonely," he suggested hopefully. "A lonesome wolf will howl all night."

"I don't think so," said Sharon, in a voice as drippy as a soggy cornflake. "Darren doesn't *ever* get lonely, Dad." She pulled a tissue from her sleeve and blew here nose. Then she wrote Darren's name in jam on her toast, took a sip of milk and sighed again.

Sharon Bunker is IN LOVE with Darren. In fact, she thinks he is a proper dreamboat. There is just something about him that sets her heart a-flutter. At school, her desk is right behind his. She sits there during lessons with her chin on her palms, staring at

Darren until her eyes go misty. She likes that sprutty bit of hair above Darren's right ear. Sometimes, it's all she can do to stop herself reaching out and . . .

SHARON! GET ON WITH YOUR WORK!

Darren, of course, completely ignores her. If Sharon so much as casts him a glance he covers his face and picks his nose. And talking to him isn't much better. Then he pulls his jumper up over his

RUMMAGE RUMMAGE

GRUNT

mouth, grunts like a gorilla and ambles away with his hands on his pockets. Once, Sharon even tried writing to him. . .

15

> Dear Darren
>
> I think you are dead, dead nice. Do you want to come and see my dad's new inventions?
>
> Lots of love
> an admirer (Sharon)
> xxxxxxxxxxxxxxxxxxxx

Darren would have loved to have seen Albert Bunker's inventions. But the thought of spending an evening near Sharon made him shiver so much his ears began to wiggle.

And so the romance seemed hopelessly doomed – until the first day of The Snail Patrol. The very same day that Sharon picked up a piece of paper that had fluttered off Darren's desk during History . . .

She'd been watching him for ages, scribbling away. Somehow she could

tell that his mind was not on Miss
Cockerill's description of the Battle of
Hastings. But it was only when Darren
stifled a giggle and Miss Cockerill
called him out to the front to explain
what was so funny about an arrow in
the eye that Sharon discovered just
what he'd been up to. She bent down
and picked the paper up. And this is
what she read . . .

She didn't understand why snails
should be so brilliant, but the message

on the paper was clear enough: so, Darren loved snails. Sharon's senses began to whirr. The Bunker brain began to invent. If Darren loved snails then perhaps she could make him a folded . . .? Or maybe if she took him a stuck-together . . .? Or better still, what if she built him a cardboard . . .? Suddenly, the bell went. Sharon folded the paper and leapt from her seat. In her excitement she forgot to blow Darren his inevitable kiss as she dashed through the classroom door that night. But it didn't matter. She had just had the most FANTASTIC idea. One that

couldn't fail to impress him. One that was bound to make him SWOON!

That night, Sharon skipped all the way home. She swung around every lamppost in the street and sang this little song over and over . . .

Slugs and snails
and puppy dogs' tails
That's what Darren is made of!

Doesn't love do funny things to some people?

# CHAPTER THREE

Meanwhile, over in Poddledown Crescent, Darren was preparing for his evening's work. It began with a rather strange request: "Mum, can we have Brussels sprouts for tea?"

Mrs Winterburn was laying the kitchen table and nearly dropped a fork on the floor in shock. "What?" she murmered. "What did you say?" It was a well-known fact that Darren hated greens.

Darren shrugged and looked out of the kitchen window. He drew a snail on the glass with his fingertip. "I just fancied some sprouts, that's all."

There was a pause. The Mrs Winterburn screeched: "Oh my goodness!" She slapped a hand to her forehead and a look of mock horror spread over her face. "Aliens have stolen my darling Darren and replaced him with an exact vegetable-eating replica! Whatever are we going to DO?!" Darren sighed. Sometimes his mother was just too daft for words.

"Anyway," she said, becoming "normal" again, "whatever you're up to, the answer is no. We're not having Brussels sprouts for tea — we're having SPINACH instead!" She prodded the tip of his nose with her finger and turned away with a satisfied smirk.

Daren was unmoved. He pulled a pen and a piece of crumply paper from his pocket. "Is spinach green and leafy?" he asked.

"Very," said his mother, taking plates from the cupboard.

Darren nodded and made a tick on the paper. "Can I have a double helping, please?"

Mrs Winterburn made a sort of squeaking noise and had to steady herself against the back of a chair. I think I might be going to faint," she said.

What Mrs Winterburn didn't know, of course, was that Darren had no intention of *eating* the spinach. He hated all veg – except carrots, possibly. If you mixed carrots with custard they were brilliant for making fake doggy sick. The spinach was just part of his MASTER PLAN. During tea, while his mum was at the fridge and his dad was filling out his football coupon, Darren snatched a big pile of spinach off his plate and squidged it carefully into his POCKET. Then, after tea, he slipped unnoticed into the garden and LOBBED the spinach over George McDuff's wall. Spinach was the perfect snail bait. Darren knew, because that afternoon he had been to the school library and looked up some interesting facts about snails.

EVERYTHING YOU EVER WANTED TO KNOW ABOUT SNAILS!

He had written them down on a page
of his workbook along with some
decent hunting tips . . .

Inturesting facts about Snails

1. Snails hide under stones (get torch, good proddy stick)

2. They come out at night in drizzuly rain (wear parka, wellies and hat)

3. They like beer (Yuk! raid Dad's secret supply in shed)

4. They eat green and leafy food (ask Mum for dubble sprouts tonight)

Darren rubbed his hands in glee.
Everything was going perfectly to plan.
It was even drizzling with rain outside
and the sky was an overcast, charcoal
grey. Now all he had to do was wait
until his mum and dad sat down to
watch TV, then he could whizz round
the house and *collect* a few things . . .

He started in the cupboard underneath the kitchen sink. That was where his mum kept her empty jamjars. Darren rooted out nine in all. He carefully put the jars and their lids in a carrier bag then opened the kitchen door and slipped, silently, out to the garage. Somewhere in the distance an owl hooted. Darren responded with a gentler howl.

To Darren's relief his dad hadn't put the car away yet, so there was plenty of room to move about in the garage. Leaving the bags of jars by the door, Darren hurried across to the shelf near the mower, opened the toolbox and rummaged around. He found a reel of string and stuffed it in his pocket. Then he lifted Dad's torch off a hook on the workbench and flashed a big round moon on the garage wall.

"*This is the voice of the Mysterons,*" he chanted. "*We have come to steal your beer, earthlings.*" He let the beam drop on to an old oak cabinet where Dad kept oil and pots of paint – and a secret supply of lager cans. Lager was a kind of beer, Darren thought. It tasted just as useless, anyway. He was wondering how much lager a snail could drink when, suddenly, the kitchen light went on. Darren panicked and pushed the torch up his jumper. If he was found in the shed with a can of lager and nine jamjars there might be some awkward explaining to do. He stood, stone-still,

and watched the house. He could see his mum at the kitchen window. She slid a few pots and pans into the bowl and tended the leaves of a spider plant. When she parted the slats of the kitchen blinds, Darren nearly shrivelled into his socks. Then, thankfully, the light went out. Darren breathed a sigh of relief. It was time he got back or he might be missed. He tiptoed towards the door of the shed, picked up the carrier bag and *clankle! clankle! clankle!* stumbled over something lying on the floor: Dad's welding goggles. Darren bit his lip. He had always wanted a go with them. They were a little bit big and they weren't reeally needed for the Snail Patrolling but . . . he snatched them up anyway. If he had to dig around in splattery mud he might be glad of some eye protection – even if he would look a total wally.

Safe in his bedroom, with his items collected, Darren became a *changed* person. Once, he had been an ordinary lad. Now he became . . .

SNAIL BOY!

# CHAPTER FOUR

It was nearly eight o'clock. Darren was
ready. He crept downstairs one step at a
time. Mum and Dad were watching a game
show on the telly. Darren tiptoed passed
the front room door and was almost clean
away when his mum's voice said:

"Where're you going, Darren?"

Darren clinked to a halt and gritted his
teeth. How did his mum *do* that? Could
all parents see through walls. Perhaps
when you grew up you got eyes in the
back of your head after all.

"I'm doing nature study, Mum – in Mr McDuff's garden."

"At this time of night?"

That was a tricky one. Darren thought hard. "Some animals only come out at night."

"Don't you bring any mice home," she said.

"Or bats," said his dad.

"Or hedgehogs," said his mother.

"Or moles," said his dad.

"Or girlfriends," teased his mother.

There was a pause. Darren heard his father laugh. "Girlfriends? At his age?"

"He's got his eye on that Sharon Bunker," said his mother.

"I FLIPPING WELL HAVEN'T!" Darren shouted. He tightened his fists and the jamjars clinked.

"What was that noise?" Mrs Winterburn said.

"I'm going," announced Darren, opening the door.

"Darren?" said his mother, "Darren, what are you up to? Darren Winterburn, you come back here."

But Darren was already at George McDuff's door.

Mr McDuff looked anxious to see him. "Come in, boy. Come in," he said in a whisper, and ushered Darren through to the back of the house. He put a finger to his lips as he slid back the huge glass patio door. The soft smell of wet earth filled the air.

"Can you hear it?" George whispered, cocking an ear towards the garden.

"What?" whispered Darren. He couldn't hear a thing.

"That scrunching," growled George. "That munching. That lunching. That cabbage-*crunching* noise. That's them, boy. They're out there. Snails. Lots of them. Ooh, it makes me so . . ."

Mad, thought Darren. Completely bonkers. "Don't worry," he said, stepping into the rain. "The Snail Patrol is at your service. Look, I've brought this." He showed George the secret can of lager.

"Och," exclaimed George, "very generous of you, laddie." And he whipped the lager from Darren's grasp. Before Darren could say that the beer was really a trap for the snails, George was guzzling it – straight from the can.

It didn't matter. The lager wasn't needed. The spinach trap had worked a treat! When Darren shone the torch into Mr McDuff's garden at least ten snails were slithering round the bait.

The first thing Darren did was take out his notepad. He had planned this bit carefully back in his room. If he kept a running tally of the snails as he caught them, it would be quicker and easier at the end of the night to work out exactly how much he was owed. He crouched beside the posse of spinach-chewing snails. Two of these were Cabbage Busters for sure. He licked his pencil and jotted down the numbers.

| TINY WORLERS (10p) | PUPPY DOG'S TAILS (20p) | CREAM TOPPERS (30p) | CATHERINE WHEELS (40p) | CABBAGE BUSTERS (50p) |
|---|---|---|---|---|
| 2 | 1 | 5 | 1 | 2 |

Eleven snails in all. Darren did a swift calculation. Three pounds thirty! He had already earned himself three pounds thirty! He picked up the tiniest Tiny Whorler and sat it sweetly on the palm of his hand. The Tiny Whorler looked confused. It had a quick peek round for non-existent spinach and slowly curled itself back into its shell.

"Night, night," said Darren with a little wave, and rolled the baby snail gently into a jar.

NIGHT, DARREN...

It was the same story all over the garden:
snails EVERYWHERE – slithering round
plant pots, crawling through the trellis,
hiding under benches, creeping
up the cold frame. Darren even
found a Whorler on a gnome's
fishing rod and a nice Cream
Topper in the outside loo! The
cabbage patch was absolutely heaving with
snails. Darren spent ages turning up the
leaves and plucking the sticky little preda-
tors off. But the best place for BIG snails
was George's dustbin. It was one of the
corrugated metal kind. It smelt horribly
of fish and cauliflower and curry, but the
snails didn't seem to mind – neither did
the woodlice. When Darren moved the bin
to unplop a Catherine Wheel from the lid,
the paving slabs were suddenly alive.

PITTER PATTER PITTER PATTER PITTER PATTER RUN FOR IT LADS!

Woodlice stampede! Darren jumped back and let go of his jar. It broke on the back of a little stone tortoise and four snails rolled into the compost heap. Darren thought about leaving them to it. But duty was duty. He didn't want any complaints from George. So he carefully put the broken glass into the dustbin, took a deep breath and shoved his hand into the compost. It was just as well he did. He found SIX snails not four, and one was the biggest Cabbage Buster he'd seen. Darren sent a jubilant howl into the night.

The Snail Patrol had done its job.

# CHAPTER FIVE

While Darren was busy celebrating his haul, about half a mile away, in a leafy little road called Cuddlup Close, Sharon Bunker and her dad were hard at work. They were in the old shed at the bottom of the garden – and something very *odd* was going on. The only clues to their behaviour were a trail of paper littering the lawn and a hose-pipe running down the garden path. Two pairs of shoes and two pairs of socks had been left out on

the lawn as well. And then there were
the noises. Strange gloopy-poopy

noises, echoing softly into the night . . .

Every now and then, there were
snatches of exciting conversation too . . .

"Gosh, Dad, my feet are getting *ever so*
sticky."

"Keep treading, Sharon. We'll soon be
there."

"Do you think he'll like it, Dad?"

"If he doesn't, he isn't worthy of you,
petal."

"He is, Dad. Honest. He's just a bit . . .
*shy*."

"Hmm – if you say so. Nip out and
get some more paper, will you?

"Can't, that bundle of comics was the last. There wasn't any more at the paper-bank either. Hhh, no paper! What are we going to do?"

"Run and get the telephone directory, Sharon."

"Why, are we going to ring someone up?"

"No, we're going to throw it in the mix!"

"Wow! A *telephone* directory?"

"Bring all the loo rolls you can find as well. More paper, Sharon! We need more paper! Tear it off the ceiling and the walls if you have to. Turn the hose on, too, I think the mix is getting dry."

"OK, Dad! Ooh, it's going to be *brilliant*, isn't it? I can't wait to see Darren's face when it's done. Tee-hee. He's going to be dead, dead gobsmacked. I wonder what he's up to – *right now*."

# CHAPTER SIX

In the garden at No. 2, Poddledown
Crescent, Darren was checking his
calculations. In just one hour he had
managed to collect twelve Tiny Whorlers,
nine Puppy Dogs' Tails, seventeen Cream
Toppers, eleven Catherine Wheels, and a
massive eighteen Cabbage Busters!
Altogether he had earned himself . . .

| TINY WORLERS (10p) | PUPPY DOG TAILS (20p) | CREAM TOPPERS (30p) | CATHERINE WHEEULS (40p) | CABBAGE BUSTERS (50p) |
|---|---|---|---|---|
| 12 | 9 | 17 | 11 | 18 |

Suddenly, the patio door slid open. "By the auld misty mountains of McCloggan," George hissed, poking his nose up close to the jars. "You've G O T them, boy! You've nabbed the beasties! The finest lot of leaf-lickers I ever did see. Well done, laddie. I'd shake you by the hand but you're full of . . ."

"Compost," explained Darren. "I had to dig a few out."

"Aye, so you would," said George with a grimace. He turned a beady eye on the snails once more. "What will you do with them now, eh, laddie? Boil them in marmarmalade and eat them on toast?"

"I don't think so," said Darren, shuddering at the thought. "I was going to let them go—"

"LET THEM GO?!" George screeched.

"In the park, Mr McDuff. It would take them years to slither back from there."

George's worried expression eased. "Aye, well, perhaps you're right. No one could eat that many toasted snails, anyway. Off you go then, boy. Afore you catch your death."

Darren started to move, then remembered he had something important to ask. "Excuse me," he said as politely as he could. "Do you think I could have my money now, please? It comes to twenty-one pounds and 50p exactly."

George McDuff turned slightly pale.

One ginger-coloured eyebrow began to twitch. "Twenty-one pounds?" he repeated in a croak.

"And 50p," said Darren proudly. "There were eighteen Cabbage Busters, Mr McDuff!" He twirled the jars round for George to see.

Mr McDuff looked thoughtfully at the snails and stroked the dark line of stubble on his chin. "Err . . . no, laddie," he haggled. "I think you might have made a *wee* mistake. A slight miscalculation, perhaps? Twenty-one pounds? It cannae be right."

"But I'm top of the class at Maths," said Darren. Under his parka his neck was feeling hot.

"Aye, maybe so," said George rather silkily, licking his lips with a tongue as slow and slimy as a snail, "but you're not terribly good at Biology, are ye?"

Darren glanced at the snail jars. "What do you mean?"

"Well, you don't know a *proper* Cabbage Buster, that's the truth of it. A real Cabbage Buster is a fearsome sight. It's an ogre-ous creature. A bloated brute. You couldnae get a giant like that in a *jar*. It would eat you up for supper, boy – wellingtons and all. No, you've made a

mistake with your reckonings. You'll have to go away and add it up again . . ."

44

"Go away?" repeated Darren. "But that means I'll have to keep the snails till tomorrow."

"Ay well," said George, "it's a problem best slept on."

"What?" protested Darren. "I can't go to sleep on sixty-seven snails!"

But George McDuff had the argument won. "Believe me, laddie, you've got it wrong. A real Cabbage Buster would gobble up the compost and spit out the lumps. It's the size of the Loch Ness Monster, for sure. Catch one of those and I'll give you fifty pounds." He grinned and pointed Darren down the side of the house.

Darren's shoulders drooped. The jamjars gave a last sad clink. "The Loch Ness Monster doesn't EXIST," he grumbled. But it made no difference. George wasn't listening. He was playing a set of imaginary bagpipes and dancing a reel all the way across the patio.

"Hmph!" Darren sniffed, and trogged off home. What a miserable night: he was wet and smelly and, worst of all, penniless; the batteries in his dad's best torch were flat; and now he had sixty-seven mouths to feed! It couldn't get much worse, he told himself.

When, in fact, it was about to get . much, much worse.

# CHAPTER SEVEN

Where to keep sixty-seven disgruntled snails? That was Darren's immediate problem as he kicked off his wellies on the kitchen step. It seemed a bit cruel to leave them squashed up in the jars. They looked like a lot of hard-boiled sweets – and they were probably gasping for air by now. Darren decided he needed a box. A box with little air holes and a fairly tight lid. A box that a big snail couldn't bite a way through.

The bread bin seemed like the perfect answer.

Darren sneaked into the kitchen and pushed back the lid. There was half a loaf of bread and two scones in the bin. He put the loaf on the breadboard and wolfed the scones down. Then, thinking the snails might be hungry, he tiptoed stealthily over to the fridge and found an old limp lettuce in the crisper compartment. He tore a few yellowed leaves into snail-sized pieces and spread the bits out on the bottom of the bin. Then he grabbed a jar. "Come on," he whispered to a dozy Cream Topper. "Teatime, look." He held the jar over the feast of lettuce. The snail, being a snail, barely managed a slither. Suddenly, from the front room, Darren heard his mother's voice: "Don't turn over, Dad, I

want to watch the weather." Darren bit his lip. He had to work fast. Mum liked a cup of tea after listening to the weather. In another five minutes she would be in the kitchen. "Come on-nn," he said again to his sleepy prisoners, and poked the snails out with the flat of a knife.

It was a close-run thing. He had just managed to put all the things back in the garage, wash his face and hands and take his parka off, when his mum came striding into the kitchen.

"Oh, there you are at last. The explorer returns. And how was your 'nature ramble' then?"

"Nature study," Darren corrected her, nudging past.

"Oh, excuse me," Mrs Winterburn huffed. "And how did your nature *study* go then? Find anything interesting in Mr McDuff's garden apart from the usual clumps of mud?"

49

"No," muttered Darren, and started up the stairs.

"Just a minute," said his mother, in that slow commanding tone that always turned Darren's spine to ice. He rested his head on the nearest riser and clawed at the fraying edges of the carpet. "I'm not a mind-reader, Darren — do you want hot chocolate or fruit juice tonight?"

Darren sighed with relief. His bedtime drink. "Chocolate, please. Can I have it in bed?"

"I suppose so," said his mother. "Do you want a scone with it? I think there might be one or two left in the—"

"No!" gasped Darren, and covered his ears.

It was awesome. Mrs Winterburn screamed so loud that plaster flaked off the kitchen ceiling. "DARRENNNNNN!" she thundered. "GET IN HERE!"

Darren inched towards the kitchen. His mother was livid. "What are those . . . *things* doing in my breadbin?"

Darren hung his head. "Resting?" he suggested. It wasn't a good answer.

"RESTING? You'll be resting across my knee!"

Darren shuffled his feet. Suddenly his denims felt remarkably thin.

"Right," said his mother, pushing up her sleeves. "First you put those *squidgers* back EXACTLY where you found them. Then you scrub every inch of this worktop until it shines so much that the sun needn't bother coming up tomorrow morning."

"But I can't, Mum!"

"WHAT?!"

"I can't put them back." Darren bit his lip hard. There was no way round it. He would have to tell his mother the truth. He took a deep gulp and gabbled the story out.

". . . so I *have* to keep them, Mum, and measure them properly – or Mr McDuff won't give me any money.

"Clever," said his dad, who had come into the kitchen when he'd heard the fuss. "Catching snails for cash. Wish I'd thought of that when I was in the Scouts."

Mrs Winterburn gave him a frosty glare.

"Dib, dib, dib," Mr Winterburn said. "Shows initiative if you want my opinion."

"I don't," said his wife. She turned to face Darren. "I have never heard anything so hare-brained in my life. I don't care how much money you're 'owed', my lad,

52

those snails are going in the garden,
NOW."

"But what if they climb up Mr McDuff's
wall?"

"Darren, I don't care if they climb up
his trouser leg and lay their eggs in his
underpants. Get them out of my kitchen.
THIS INSTANT!" Mrs Winterburn
pointed fiercely at the door.

With a defeated sigh Darren hoisted
the bread bin off the worktop, walked to
the door and yanked it
open. "And another
thing," Mrs Winterburn
snapped. Darren teetered
on the kitchen step.
"You can throw that
bread bin away when
you've finished. We
won't be needing it any
more . . ."

What? thought Darren. Chuck out the bread bin? Did that mean no more bread, ever? No more sugar sandwiches? No more beans on toast? No more soldiers for his hard-boiled eggs? Surely his mum couldn't be so cruel?

But Mrs Winterburn hadn't quite finished . . .

". . . because on Saturday morning, you and I are going into town and you are going to buy *me* a brand-NEW bread bin.'

Darren blinked, confused. "I haven't got any money, Mum."

"Oh yes you have. You've got the Christmas money Auntie Alison gave you."

"But MUM!" Darren whipped around. He was going to put that money towards a pair of trainers or a Manchester United football jersey.

"Go," said his mother, pointing garden-wards.

54

"Oh fff!" Darren stamped and kicked the door wide. Behind him, something crashed to the floor.

"And you can add an egg-timer to the list as well!" Mrs Winterburn thundered through the kitchen window.

That was it, Darren decided. Grown-ups were ROTTEN. They only existed to make his life a misery. He was sure they kept a secret plan somewhere. "Get Darren." That was probably all it said.

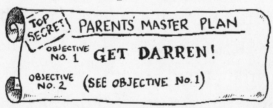

Well he was going to get his own back, that much was certain. No one *swizzled* *him* out of his Christmas money. He mooched down the garden with the bread bin tucked underneath his arm and thoughts of revenge piling up in his mind.

Where had Dad planted those geranium flowers? The ones they'd bought for Mother's Day? If he tipped the snails out there they would eat the geraniums and Mum couldn't complain because it was HER IDEA. She'd be sorry when all she had was STALKS in the morning.

"Don't be all night!" his mum bellowed from the kitchen.

Darren stuck out his tongue – but got a move on, anyway. It was cold and the rain was drizzling in his face. He squelched across the lawn to the flower-bed nearest the garden pond. To his dismay there was nothing but wet earth and pebbles in the bed. Not so much as a single leaf. He

frowned and kicked a plastic gnome into the pond.

"Are you done?" yelled his mother.

"No," Darren yelled back, looking around. There had to be *somewhere* decent for the snails. And then he saw it: the gap in the fence: a football-sized hole in the wooden slats. "Come on," he told the snails, "you're going on holiday." And one by one he dropped them through the hole – into Mrs Dumpity's vegetable plot, at No. 6, Poddledown Crescent . . .

# CHAPTER EIGHT

It was a while before Darren got to sleep
that night. He sat on the end of his bed
for ages, doing snail tattoos on the cover
of his workbook and thinking up ways
to get his own back on George.

By the time he finally curled up inside
his duvet, he had come up with several
interesting possibilities:

58

1. Paint butterflies on George's cabbages.
2. Throw compost at his ~~patted~~ big glass doors.
3. Crack a rotten egg in his dussbin.
4. Train Mrs Dumpity's cat to do its doings in his garden (insted of ours)
5. Make some SLIME

It was the last of these he settled on. In the morning, while his mum was in the shower and his dad was having a shave, Darren nipped into the shed and dug out a bucket. Overnight, he had concocted a dastardly plan. A plan so slippery, so gooey, so globby that the sheer STICKI-NESS of it made him shudder. It was a plan that depended on a number of things: nerves, timing, the biggest paint-brush he could possibly find and several first-class *bucketloads* of goo. Everything depended on the quality of the slime.

But would he be able to make it properly?
In his workbook, he had jotted down a
hopeful recipe:

> Darren's Slime:
> Mix ten squirts of washing-up
> likwid with half a can of
> kustard, four banananas, some
> porrige, some lemunade and
> some spit. Stir well or tread
> mixture hard with feet. (Take
> socks off first)

Darren mixed some up in the bucket. It
was absolutely useless. It looked like some
thing a dog had yakked up. It
was lumpy and yellow and it
bubbled and glopped like an
alien amoeba. Darren folded
his arms and kicked the bucket in disgust.
The bucket toppled over and the mess
spilled, fortunately, into the drain. Darren
washed it away and got ready for school.

Despite the setback, Darren was determined. He was going to get George and he needed slime. If *he* couldn't make it, he would have to get the help of someone who could. Darren gulped and his arms came up in goosebumps. There was only one person he could really think of. Someone in his class. Sharon Bunker.

Sharon was a genius at arts and crafts. She had once built a miniature orbital space station entirely out of milk bottle tops. It was hanging in the classroom above Miss Cockerill's desk. If anyone could mix up slime, it would be Sharon.

Darren found her in the playground at morning break. She was singing to herself as she often did and drawing chalk hearts on the dinner-room wall.

Darren squirmed when he saw his name in one. He approached with caution: "Oi, freckle face."

Sharon turned round. "Darren," she breathed. The stick of chalk shattered into pieces on the ground.

Darren lifted his jumper up over his mouth. "Want to ask you something," he muttered through the fabric.

"Do you?" Sharon gasped. Her eyes were like moons.

"If you laugh, I'll tie you to the gates by your hair."

"I won't laugh," Sharon promised, and drew a shaky finger across her heart.

Darren swallowed hard. He pulled his

jumper up to cover his nose. "How d'you make slime?"

"Hhh!" gasped Sharon. Her eyes lit up. She leaned forward a little. Darren immediately leaned twice as far back. "Muddy brown slime or green snaily slime?"

Darren shifted his gaze first left, then right. "Snaily slime," he answered carefully.

"Thought so," Sharon whispered, risking a smile. Darren stared at her hard. She looked at her feet.

"You'll need a bucket," she said.

"I know *that*," Darren tutted.

"And some washing-up liquid, some bananas, some milk and . . . and . . . I can't think of the other thing.

"Porridge?" suggested Darren.

"No!" Sharon laughed.

She clamped her hands tightly across her mouth.

Darren gritted his teeth. "What other thing?"

"I'll think of it," she said. "I'll tell you in class."

As it happened, Sharon managed to tell EVERYONE in class. Halfway through English, Miss Cockerill spotted her passing a note. Darren had to go up and read it aloud. It said:

Dear Darren
  Please come and talk to me again tomorrow. Please, please, please, please PLEASE. You are dead handsome, even with your face tucked into your jumper. Your best friend Sharon xxx.
                    P.S. You need some GUNKO

"Ooooooh!" went the class. "Sharon loves Darren! Please, Miss, what's GUNKO?"

Darren groaned and buried his face in his workbook.

# CHAPTER NINE

The next day was Saturday. Shopping day. When his alarm went off Darren slid beneath the covers and made himself as flat as he possibly could. "Goodness," said his mother when she came into the room. "Darren seems to have completely disappeared. Oh well, it'll give me the chance to wash these sheets." And with a mighty tug she pulled everything off the bed, Darren included.

"Up," she growled, "we're going shopping."

In Whattley's Wonderful World of Hardware, Mrs Winterburn was in her element. She didn't make for the bread bins straight away. Instead, she tortured Darren with a dreadful tour of clothes pegs, dusters, mops, candles, picture frames, plastic plates, can-openers . . . and egg-timers. The most painful bit of all was when they looked for a birthday card for Darren's Grandad Potter. Mrs Winterburn examined THOUSANDS of cards and went "aah" at all the stupid rhymes. Darren was SO BORED he nearly fell asleep in a wire basket full of special-offer cushions. By the time they had made it to the kitchenware shelves he was ready to hand over every penny of his Christmas money just to be able to get back on the bus. And then, as if things weren't bad enough already, something really GHASTLY happened: who should turn up, but Sharon Bunker.

She was wandering down the aisle, staring up at the shelves. Mrs Winterburn was actually the first to see her. "Sharon," she cooed. Darren and Sharon looked up together. Their eyes met. Sharon made a noise like a puppy dog looking for somewhere to wee wee. Darren felt the blood draining into his toes.

"Doing a spot of decorating?" Mrs Winterburn chirped. "Grey, green and brown. That's an interesting choice of colours."

Sharon bit her lip. She glanced at the tins of paint in her basket then switched the basket from one hand to the other. "No," she muttered, "I'm . . . making something."

"Something nice?" said Mrs Winterburn.

"What?" said Sharon.

"Are you making something nice? A present for someone?"

Sharon shuftied her feet so her toes pointed inwards. She glanced awkwardly at
Darren and shook her head.

"Fine," said Mrs Winterburn in quiet exas-
peration. She'd had easier conversations
with the plants in her lounge. "Well, shall
I tell you what *we're* doing here?"

"No!" Darren blurted out, shooting
daggers at his mum.

"Darren is buying me a brand-new
bread bin."

"Is he?" said Sharon, picking up inter-est. "Is it your birthday, then, Mrs Winterburn?"

Mrs Winterburn shook her head. "Tell her, Darren. Tell Sharon all about it. Tell her what you put in the *old* bread bin."

Darren's shoulders slumped. Right at that moment he could have happily crawled into the nearest flip-top bin. But it was useless to protest. His mother had already folded her arms. It was a sign that said "you will not get out of here unless you do as I command". Darren pulled his jumper up over his chin.

"Snails," he mumbled.

There was a breathless pause. Then, to Darren's surprise, Sharon gulped and took a stumbling pace backwards. "Got to go," she said urgently. Her eyes were aflame.

"Oh," said Mrs Winterburn, frowning slightly. "Well, I'd like to say it's been nice talking to you, Sha—"

But Sharon was gone. With a hitch to her dungarees she had turned and scooted away down the aisle. At the end of the aisle she skidded to a halt, looked left, looked right, looked back at Darren, bit her lip once then shot off in the direction of the checkouts.

"Strange child," Mrs Winterburn muttered.

Darren didn't answer. He was still in a daze. That was the second time in two days he'd spoken to Sharon. He would have to be careful: too many close encounters might bring him out in some sort of rash.

70

He glanced around to see if Whattley's had a medical section, just in case – and that was when a notice caught his eye.

It was a large advertisement – a Whattley's special offer – and it was advertising just what Darren NEEDED. He started to make his way towards it, but his mother caught his arm and pulled him back.

"Don't run off."

Darren looked up. There were bread bins everywhere.

"Now then, what do you think?" said his mum. "Shall we have this one with the roses on it? Or is the colour going to clash with the kitchen paper? These wooden

ones are nice, but they're quite expensive. Still, I could always take an extra two pounds from your pocket money . . ."

Darren's mind worked fast. He glanced at the advert, then at the prices of the various bread bins. "Can we buy the one with the roses on, Mum?"

Mrs Winterburn gave him a searching look. "Good Lord. You almost said that as if you meant it."

Darren slid his hands into the pockets of his jeans. "If I buy you the one with the roses on, Mum, there'll be five pounds left of my Christmas money. Can I spend the change on something for Dad's Day?"

Mrs Winterburn blinked. She laid her hand against Darren's brow. "Hmm, no fever" she said, a bit ungraciously. "Well, Darren, I'm stunned. That's a very noble thought. What is it you want to buy for your dad?"

Darren grabbed a basket and shot off towards the sign. A moment later he was back. "This," he said proudly, holding up a round red plastic tub. "The stuff he cleans his hands with when he's been  working on the car!"

Mrs Winterburn tapped her foot on the floor. "Darren, that only costs 50p. What about the other four pounds 50p?"

Darren gave his mother a sheepish grin and dangled the basket in front of her nose.

There were nine other tubs of Gunko in it.

# CHAPTER TEN

That night, Darren had a terrible dream. In it he could hear someone calling his name. The voice had a distant, muffled ring and seemed to be floating all through the house. Darren dreamed he got out of bed and opened his wardrobe. There was nothing there. He checked his cupboard. Nothing there either (except a smelly pair of underpants). Then Darren remembered a trick he had seen in a spy film once: if you held an empty tumbler against a wall and put your ear to the base of the tumbler, you could easily hear sounds from the room next door. Darren didn't have a tumbler. But he did have a mug of drinking chocolate. Quickly, he tipped the chocolate into his shoes, put the mug to the floor and listened through that.

"*Darren*," wailed the voice. "*Darren, down here* . . ." Darren gulped and started to quake. The voice was floating up from the kitchen. A soppy sort of voice that made his ears wiggle. There was only one person who could do that to him. But what was Sharon Bunker doing in the house?

Just then, the dream switched and Darren was downstairs. He was standing in the kitchen in his Snail Patrol outfit. Sharon Bunker was nowhere to be seen, but something peculiar was happening to the bread bin. It was blowing up like a huge balloon. It rattled on the worktop and flipped on to its lid. Slimy-green *slimy* stuff oozed through the air holes.

"**Darren**," said the floaty voice, "*give us a hand . . .*"

Darren quaked in his wellingtons. The voice was coming from inside the bin! The bread bin wobbled and fell to the floor. Darren 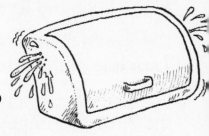 shut his eyes – and soon wished he hadn't. When he opened them again the bin was the size of the washing machine! Any moment now it was going to burst! Darren needed to act. He grabbed an egg beater off the rack on the wall. "Go away!" he shouted, and beat the bin hard.

Bad mistake.

With a thunderous

the bin exploded. And out of the debris grew . . .

"Oh no," gasped Darren, stumbling back.

The giant snail uncoiled itself. It tilted its slimy grey head to one side, wiggled its horns and rudely burped. **"Oh, *there you are*,"** it said, smiling at him.

Darren screamed. The snail had Sharon's face! Freckles, fuzzy hair, soppy eyes – the lot!

"*Cor, I'm ever so hungry,*" it said, poking its stubby nose around the kitchen. It tipped up a half-empty biscuit barrel and sniffed at a packet of honey-flavoured cereals. Neither seemed to appeal to it much. Then it spotted the vegetable rack.

"*Cabbages!*" it grunted, and promptly wolfed the lot.

That was the moment Darren woke up.

"Sharon, don't eat me!" he jabbered

through his spit. He sat bolt upright and nearly bashed his dad on the chin in the process.

"Darren, are you feeling all right?" asked his dad. "You were shouting 'cabbages' at the top of your voice.

"It's the Cabbage Buster, Dad! She's come to get me!"

"Now, Darren, that's no way to talk about your mother. I'm off to football straight after breakfast. If you want to come and watch, you'll have to get up now."

"Can't, Dad. I've got things to do."

"What things?" said Mr Winterburn.

"Things," said Darren.

Lovely, sticky, gooey things. Sharon Bunker's recipe for slime had WORKED. The addition of a tub of Gunko to the mixture had made the slime just slithery and slippery enough. Half an hour after

his dad had gone to football, Darren
decided to test it out. He dug out the
biggest paintbrush he could find and
smeared a trail of slime on the garage
floor. It didn't look much with the
garage door closed. But an hour later
when his dad came home and swung the
door up to put the car away, a beam of
sunlight fell across the trail and gave it
that snaily, glistening look. Darren was
delighted. Mr Winterburn less so . . .

"What on earth is *this*?" he said, pacing
along the length of the trail.
Darren was standing in a corner of the
garage, blowing up a ball with a bicycle

pump. "Dunno," he shrugged, and carried on pumping.

Mr Winterburn crouched and put a finger in the slime. "Ugh, it feels like . . . Gunko," he grimaced.

Darren closed his eyes and said a silent prayer. If word of this reached his mother's ears it could mean no pocket money for about four years.

Mr Winterburn rubbed the slime between his fingers. He brought it up to his nose and sniffed. "And it smells like . . ."

Darren pumped like mad and tried not to listen. He wondered what the options were if he had to leave home.

"Don't know, can't place it," Mr Winterburn decided. He stood up, puzzled, and followed the trail outside. "It seems to be heading straight for the hedge." There was a pause. Darren's heartbeat hammered at his ribs. Then, very slowly, Mr Winterburn said: "Darren, you know those snails you collected, what *exactly* did you do with them? Because if I didn't know better, I'd say this was a giant SNAIL TRAIL . . ."

"YES!" Darren whooped, giving the air a punch. The ball shot off the end of the pump, bounced down the drive and rolled under the hedge.

"Throw my ball back, Dad," Darren said chirpily, busy with a dance of celebration.

Mr Winterburn strode forward to look for the ball, then changed his mind and stopped dead in his tracks. "Erm . . . well, it erm. . ." He stood back and wagged a finger at the hedge. "You get it," he gulped. "It's your ball, isn't it?" He shuddered slightly and stretched out his chin.

"Aw, Dad, you're nearer," Darren protested, wondering what all the fuss was about. Then, suddenly, the answer dropped into place. His dad didn't want to look for the ball because he didn't want to go too close to the hedge. There might be a giant SNAIL lurking there. Mr Winterburn was stalling. He was *scared*.

"A-woooooooooooo!" Darren howled and stretched his arms to the sky.

It was time to track down George McDuff.

# CHAPTER ELEVEN

That afternoon, the weather was glorious.
Just the sort of day for a poddle down the
Crescent. Shortly after lunch of boiled
beans and cabbage – *fresh* cabbage,
*unchewed by snails* – George stepped out
for his Sunday walk. He swept along at a
good brisk pace, swinging his stick as if
conducting the birdsong and whistling
an aged Scottish ballad. In a matter of
minutes he was clear of the houses and
striding down the path that rounded the
allotments. Ahhhh! He took a deep and

snorty breath. Peace and quiet. You couldnae beat it. No noise. No fuss. And definitely no snails.

But there was Darren Winterburn.

He came shooting along the allotment path, waving and flapping as if his hair was on fire. George scowled and drilled his stick into the ground. For the last two days he'd managed to avoid any contact with the boy. The scamp was going to badger him for money, no doubt.

But Darren had other things on his mind.

"Did you see it?" he panted, skidding to a halt in front of George.

George looked around. There wasn't so much as a leaf falling.

"I think it might be hiding in the spinney," Darren puffed, pointing at a distant clump of trees.

George McDuff cupped a hand across his eyes. There was nothing but scrub from th path to the spinney. "What in blazes are you talking of, laddie?"

"The SNAIL!" Darren shouted. "The Cabbage Buster!"

Mr McDuff hopped back a pace.

"I saw it," said Darren. "At least I *think* I did. It wasn't as big as the Loch Ness monster, but I could see its shell curling out of the grass. It was an OGRE-OUS creature, Mr McDuff. I bet it's miles away by now.

George McDuff straightened up very slowly. "Aye, it probably is," he agreed. "I expect it sprouted wings and FLEW!" He nearly spat the last word into Darren's face

"You'll have to do better to fool McDuff! I wasnae born in a haystack, you know!"

Darren put on his best hurt look. "I wasn't trying to fool you, Mr McDuff."

Mr McDuff shook his stick at the boy. "It's a crafty, thieving trick," he said. "You want me to give you fifty pounds – all for a creature that doesnae EXIST!"

Which was just what Darren had expected to hear. "But you told me there WAS a Cabbage Buster!" he argued.

George gritted his teeth and said something fusty under his breath.

"If there isn't, I want my money!" Darren pressed. He held out his hand. "Twenty-one pounds and 50p please."

"No," said George.

Right, thought Darren, you asked for it.

It was time to put "Operation Slime" into action. "Ugh, what's that?" He pointed downwards.

"Uh?" George grunted, and turned around. There on the ground was a terrible sight. Weaving a ragged path through the grass was a thick, glistening, silvery-green trail. "Nay," George muttered, "it cannae be . . ." He looked towards the spinney and his teeth began to chatter.

"Wow!" exclaimed Darren, coming to crouch by the trail. "So it's true: I *did* see

a Cabbage Buster. Cor, I wonder what it's doing round here? Perhaps it comes to feed on the allotments? I can't see many cabbages growing. Perhaps it's had them all already . . ."

There was a hasty scrabbling of feet on the path. Darren pretended not to hear. "I hope it doesn't go looking for some in your back garden, Mr McDuff . . ."

Darren paused and looked over his shoulder. The gangly figure of George McDuff was already just a dwindling shape in the distance.

"Heh heh, got you," Darren laughed, licking his finger and ticking the air. He sidled across to an old tree stump and waited until George was completely out of sight. **"Dar-run! Dar-run!"** he chanted cockily – and picked up his empty bucket of slime.

# CHAPTER TWELVE

That night, Darren was in a buoyant mood. Stage one of "Operation Slime" had gone as smoothly as a snail up a lollipop. George was already a gibbering wreck - and the best part hadn't even started yet! Darren put his hand in his empty pocket. Soon it would be loaded with fifty-pence coins. He slipped on his parka and hurried to the garage to pick up his trusty slime brush and bucket. He was going to need lots of glop tonight. Good job there were plenty of bananas in the fruit bowl.

About seven o'clock there was a knock on George's door. George opened it a crack. Darren was there. "Mr McDuff! I've seen another one!" he panted, pretending he had just come running down the road.

"Another what?" George hissed.

"Another *trail*," stressed Darren. "It's HUGE! It's just at the end of the Crescent. It goes round and round the trees and in and out the gardens. The big snail must have got a whiff of something. I hope it's not your CABBAGE PATCH."

George McDuff pulled the door wide open. He craned his neck and peered up the Crescent. "N-n-nay," he tremored. "I cannae see a thing."

"But Mr McDuff, it's *there*. I've *seen* it. If you don't believe me, come and have a look."

Darren thrust out his arm to point the way – and that was the moment disaster struck. Something hit the drive with a gentle *splat!* Darren and George looked down together. A glob of slime was sitting on the Tarmac. A tell-tale blob of snaily substance. Darren blinked and turned his head to look at his arm. A trickle of Gunko was running down his wrist. Drat, how could he have been so STUPID? He still had the slime brush in his HAND!

"Erm," he muttered, backing off a pace. He switched the brush from one hand to the other and wiped his wrist on the leg of his jeans. "I think I ought to go back and keep a lookout . . ."

"Aye," said George, putting two and two together, "someone should keep a lookout, all right."

Darren bit his lip and back-pedalled some more. Was it too late to go through with his plan? "If you like, I could guard your gate, Mr McDuff - just in case the Cabbage Buster comes down the Crescent?"

"Aye," said George, stepping forwards, a dark look festering in his squinty eyes. "Maybe you could BASH it. Maybe you could TRASH it. Maybe you could SMASH it to slithereens!"

Darren gulped and nearly stumbled over some pebbles. "It only costs 50p an hour," he blurted. "Or a pound if I have to do

93

Saturday afternoons . . ."

"I'll give ye 50p an hour!" George roared and lowering his head he charged at Darren like a bony rhino.

"I'd make sure your cabbages were safe!" Darren squeaked, turning and running towards the gate.

"Get OUT!" cried George. "You're a thief. You're a robber. You're a cheating scoundrel and no mistake!"

"You owe me my Snail Patrol money!" Darren shouted.
But he wasn't going to hang around and argue about it.

☆ ☆ ☆

Darren was mad. *Hopping* mad. He swept into the kitchen like a tidal wave, banged the door shut, stamped his feet, toe-poked the fridge and slumped at the table with his head on his arms.

"Darren's home!" his mother announced gaily, sliding pots into the washing-up bowl.

"Shut up," said Darren in a muffled voice.

"So glad to know you still love me," said his mum. "Don't go and get yourself settled there. Unless by some remarkable chance you want to help me set the table?"

"No," Darren sulked.

"Worth a try," said his mother. "Well, tea won't be ready for another half hour. Go out and terrorize the neighbourhood some more. I'm sure you can think of something to do."

There was a pause. Then Darren sat up smartly. "I can," he snapped, and dashed out as quickly as he'd just dashed in.

"Yes, 'bye Mum'," Mrs Winterburn sighed, and reached for the bottle of washing-up liquid. She squeezed. It sneezed. A bubble popped weakly out of the spout. "Hmm, not you as well?" she tutted, and wrote *w. up lqd.* on her shopping reminder – underneath *milk* and *b'nas* (underlined).

DR'NK CHOC
CUST'D
LEM'NADE
SP'NCH
T'RCH BATT.
MILK
B'NAS
W. UP LQD.

# CHAPTER THIRTEEN

It was going to be Darren's final stand. He didn't care how much trouble he might get into. He was going to make a STATEMENT. And what a statement. A crushing REVELATION. A message of PROTEST to the whole wide world (well, the residents of Poddledown Crescent, anyway). He only hoped he had enough slime in his bucket.

He began it on the pavement by George McDuff's hedge:

At least, that was what he intended to put. As it happened, he didn't get all the way through it. He was finishing the loop on the bottom of the pound sign when he took a step backwards – and bumped into something.

"Sorry," said Darren.

"*Cabbages!*" said the something.

Darren stood bolt upright and dropped his brush. "*Cabbages?*" he mouthed, and looked over his shoulder.

"*Hello,*" said the giant snail.

"Aaaghh!" cried Darren – and started to run.

He ran without knowing where he was going – straight to the end of Poddle-

down Crescent, round the corner into Bobbalong Drive, then a quick sharp left up Tootle Road. He ran so fast his lungs were hurting. But if there was one thing Darren knew about snails, it was that snails never did anything fast.

This snail was different. This snail could MOTOR. It was never more than a few metres behind him and several times it drew alongside.

"*Stop*," it kept saying.

"No way!" screamed Darren, and turned, without thinking, down Orchards Alley. Orchards Alley was a DEAD END. Darren skidded to a halt.

He had nowhere to go. The snail had him trapped against a solid brick wall with high wooden fences to either side. And there was no hope of running back the way he'd come because the snail was almost as wide as the alley. What was the Cabbage Buster going to do?

It sneezed – like a little flock of sparrows taking off. Every strand of Darren's hair stood straight to attention.

"*Sorry,*" said the snail.

"S'all right," Darren squeaked.

"*Cabbages!*" it said. "*You don't half run fast.*"

"So do you," Darren tremored. "Please

don't eat me."

"Ugh," the snail giggled, "I *wouldn't do* THAT. *Little boys are made of puppy dogs' tails. Imagine eating a plateful of* THEM."

Darren grinned and made a sort of whimpering noise. If he remembered the rhyme correctly, little boys were made of SLUGS and SNAILS and puppy dogs' tails. But he didn't think he ought to tell the Cabbage Buster that. He tried to look past it, to shout for help. The Cabbage Buster dipped and swivelled its head.

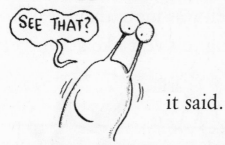 it said.

"What?" squealed Darren, throwing himself so flat against the wall he could have been painted on to the bricks.

"*I can move my head any way I like. Up,*

down and side to side. Good, isn't it?"

"Brilliant," said Darren, turning his face away. The beast was toying with him, surely? Any minute now it was going to squdge him or whatever giant snails usually did with their prey.

The giant snail coughed. Darren winced. His fingernails clawed for a hold on the bricks.

"Are you all right?" said the snail. "You look a bit . . . peaky. I hope you're not going to get my cold."

Peaky? Darren was more than peaky. He was starting to sweat like a lump of

MAYBE IF
I TELL IT
I'M SORRY...

cheese. He couldn't take much more of this. Perhaps if he just said sorry for the Snail Patrol, the Cabbage Buster might leave him alone?

"I didn't mean it!" he blurted. "Honestly, I didn't. It was Mr McDuff who wanted me to do it!"

"*Do what?*" said the snail. "*Have you got a tissue?*"

"No," Darren tutted, a bit put out. What was it about this snail? Perhaps it snotted its victims to death. He tried again. "I'm sorry I squashed your friends into jars."

"*Jars?*" said the snail, with a giant-sized sniff.

"Jamjars," said Darren, getting tetchier by the second. Honestly, this snail was completely thick. "Isn't that why you're after me? You want to get revenge because I caught a lot of snails, put them into jars and asked Mr McDuff to pay for them?"

"Wha-at?" said the snail, rearing slightly.

"Help!" squealed Darren, closing his eyes. "I'll never do it again, I promise. Please don't squdge me. I'm a nice boy, really."

"I know," said the snail, in a soppy sort of voice.

Darren opened one eye. Hang on a minute. He knew that voice. It was the one that made his ears start to wiggle! He opened both eyes and stared HARD at the snail. The Cabbage Buster tilted its head rather shyly. For the first time, Darren noticed that the skin of the snail didn't seem as leathery as it ought to. If anything, it looked rather rigid and clean. Painted even. A painted snail? He lifted a finger and touched its neck. It felt a bit like . . . *papier mâché*.

Darren folded his arms and scowled. "Boo!" he went loudly, up the snail's nose.

"Waah!" went the snail and nearly

104

toppled over.

"Cabbages!" snapped Darren.

"*Sprouts!*" it laughed.

"Fake!" Darren shouted, and rapped his

knuckles on the Cabbage Buster's nose.
There was a sharp, hollow knocking sound.

"*Tee-hee, didn't feel a thing,*" it said.

Darren stormed down the snail's side.
"Where are you?" he shouted. "I know
you're in there! How do you get in? Come
out! NOW!"

There was silence a moment. The snail
seemed to know the game was up. "*Promise
not to pull my hair?*" it said.

"NO!" said Darren.

"*Just a minute,*" said the snail. Slowly it reversed to the end of the alley. There

was a click and a door swung open in its shell. Darren stood back and gasped in amazement.

"I knew it! I knew it was you!" he stamped.

Sharon climbed off her bike and stood beside him. "I only did it because you liked snails."

"I HATE snails!" cried Darren. "I hate them! I hate them!"

Sharon stroked the snail's neck and

looked a bit miffed. "But I saw you drawing some in class, *and* you asked me how to make slime."

"I hate slime TOO!"

"But why?" said Sharon.

Darren sighed and stubbed his toe against the ground. "You'll laugh," he said.

"I won't," said Sharon, crossing her heart. She sat on a low wall and patted the space beside her. Darren slumped down – and told her everything.

"But that's terrible!" said Sharon a few minutes later. "You've been swizzled! Mr McDuff ought to pay you the money!"

"I know *that*," Darren grouched, "but how can I make him?"

Sharon thought hard. She glanced at her snail.

And a strange sort of smile lit up her face.

# CHAPTER FOURTEEN

About half an hour later there was another loud knock on George McDuff's door. George opened it a crack. Sharon was there.

"Excuse me," she said. "I'm looking for a boy called Darren Winterburn. I don't suppose you've seen him, have you?"

Mr McDuff eyed Sharon suspiciously. "You ought to be ashamed of yourself, wee lassie, making up with a rogue like that."

Sharon put on her best worried look.

"But he's disappeared," she said. "Completely vanished. He said he was going on a snail hunt tonight. He said he'd seen a giant snail round here somewhere. He said it was leaving big trails everywhere."

"Did he now?" said George, peering beadily round the garden. "Aye, I think I see one just over there." He pointed away over Sharon's head. All along the drive was a massive trail. It started at the gate, looped twice round George's circular flower-bed and continued on down the side of the house.

"Follow me," George beckoned, grinding his teeth. "I think you'll find what you're looking for down here . . ."

Sharon glanced at the trail and seemed a bit hesitant. "I don't want to get eaten by a giant snail."

"Hah!" George grizzled, stomping down the drive. "I dinnae know how you've got the nerve to play along with it. You ought tae be ashamed – trying to trick an auld man. There's no such thing as a giant SNAIL!"

Sharon smiled and tapped her fingertips together. *"That's what you think,"* she whispered to herself. *"Three, two, one. . ."*

George's scream came right on cue. "Help! It's the Cabbage Buster!" he yelped, jumping up and down and pulling out his hair. "It's got ma cabbages – and it's got the BOY!"

"Oh dear," said Sharon, "so it has."

There in the garden was the giant snail.
On the ground in front of it were several
cabbage leaves. In front of the leaves were
Darren's trainers.

"He's been gobbled!" George wittered.
"Snacked by a snail!"

"Tch!" went Sharon. "And he'd
promised to help me with my homework
as well!"

"*Cabbages!*" said the snail, and came
trundling forwards. George McDuff
screamed and didn't hang about. He
turned and ran – *smack!* into his garden
gate.

"Ooh, sorry," said Sharon. "I closed that."

"Mercy!" George jabbered, and shot
down the garden – with the Cabbage
Buster in hot pursuit.

It chased him everywhere
– up and down the cabbage
patch, in and out the flower-
beds, four times round
the compost heap. Sharon stood
on the patio and whooped with
laughter. And then, suddenly, it
all went wrong. On the third
and final circuit of the garden, Mr McDuff managed
to leap over the pond.

"Darren, no!" cried Sharon
as the snail tried to follow.

There was a sproing! and a splash.

The snail stopped moving. It tottered
slightly, then tottered some more. *"Help!"*
it cried and toppled right over.
A blue-socked foot splattered about in
the pond.

"Oh, Darren," sighed Sharon. "Now
we're for it."

As if by magic, the gate latch sounded.
Mrs Winterburn came hurrying into the
garden. "What on EARTH is going on?"
she bellowed. She glared at Sharon,

frowned at George, saw the feet protruding from the base of the snail and seemed to work everything out at once. "Right," she said, and pushed up her sleeves.

She was at the snail's side in five angry strides. She found the door, opened it, grabbed Darren by the ear and yanked him out. "You'd better have a good excuse for this, Darren Winterburn!"

Darren looked at Sharon. "Sorry," he mumbled, "it was hard to pedal without my trainers."

"I'll give you trainers," his mother growled. "Get used to slippers. You're staying in your room for at least a week!"

"No!" Sharon protested. "It's all my fault. Take me, Mrs Winterburn! I plotted it all!"

"Sharon, SHUT UP," Mrs Winterburn said.

"Yes, Mrs Winterburn," Sharon said meekly.

Mrs Winterburn turned to Darren. "Now," she said, hovering over him. "First you apologize to Mr McDuff and then . . . Where is Mr McDuff by the way?" Everyone looked around. George McDuff had completely disappeared. Then down the garden a deep voice rasped:

"*Cabbages! Ha, ha!*"

The snail was out of the garden pond and doing a few wobbly circles on the lawn. But there was something very different about it now: it seemed to have acquired a Scottish accent.

"Oh good grief . . ." Mrs Winterburn groaned. Darren and Sharon just burst out laughing.

Just then, Darren's dad appeared on the scene. "Wow," he said, "that snail's fantastic!"

"Aye," said George, "it's a brilliant feat of engineering. Would you take twenty-five pounds for it?"

"WHAT?" gasped Darren's parents together.

"If this doesn't keep the little munchers at bay, nothing will," George said triumphantly.

"I think he wants to use it as a scarecrow," said Darren.

"I think he wants his head seeing to," Mrs Winterburn added.

"I think we want fifty pounds," Sharon muttered. "It'll cost you FIFTY pounds!"

she shouted.

"Fifty *pounds?*" Mr Winterburn squawked.

Sharon nodded. "That's what he offered for a Cabbage Buster." She turned to the snail again. "Plus the twenty-one pounds 50p you owe Darren from before!"

Darren blinked at Sharon. George would never agree to *that*.

There was a momentary pause, then the Cabbage Buster said:

*"Aye, it's a bargain. But I'm a wee bit short of change right now. Could you see your way clear to accepting a cheque?"*

Sharon clapped her hands and beamed at Darren. Darren beamed back double.

He was in LOVE!

# CHAPTER FIFTEEN

This time, George paid up without a murmur. And everyone, even Darren's mum, was happy. Even she admitted things had worked out well: she had her bread bin; Darren's dad had a lifetime's supply of Gunko; Mr McDuff had his snail deterrent; Darren had his money; and Sharon . . . had Darren!

Darren was very grateful indeed. He offered to split the money with Sharon. Sharon, after all, had forfeited her bike when the snail was sold to Mr McDuff. But Sharon said Darren could keep the money – as long as he promised to stay her friend and not waste it all on sweets or chocolate. Darren said he'd buy a goalkeeper's jersey. Sharon thought he'd look very nice in that.

And incredibly, that wasn't the end of the saga. While Darren and Sharon were washing away the trails they had made in the Crescent, Mrs Dumpity came shuffling up.

She tapped Darren on the shoulder. "Snails," she said.

Darren nearly gagged. "Where?" he whispered.

"Slithering all over my vegetable plot."

Darren's face turned scarlet. The hole in the fence. The night of the bread bin came back to haunt him. And yet Mrs Dumpity didn't seem angry.

"Turned up like visitors from outer space," she muttered. "Never had them in those sorts of numbers before. I was talking to your father yesterday, Darren. He says you offer some kind of service?"

Darren looked at Sharon. The Bunker brain was already at work.

"It's called the Snail Patrol," she said with a grin. "We charge 10p to collect the smallest ones and 50p for the biggest."

"It's a sliding scale," Darren put in, trying his hardest to keep a straight face.

"Sounds very reasonable," Mrs Dumpity said. "I'll expect you both tonight, then. Kettle's on at eight." And with that, she poddled off down the Crescent.

"Yes-ss!" Darren cheered, dancing on the pavement. " Brilliant! We're going to be RICH!"

"Hmm, Sharon nodded, deep in thought. She came up and linked her arm through his. "Listen, I've got an idea," she whispered, and made him walk down the Crescent with her. "When we've caught the snails in Mrs Dumpity's garden, let's empty them in Mrs Mangleweed's."

"What for?" said Darren.

"You are thick," Sharon tutted. "Because then Mrs Mangleweed will pay us to catch them and we can drop them in Mr Nicely's front. Then Mr Nicely will pay us to catch them and . . . how many houses are there in the Crescent?"

"Twenty-eight," grinned Darren, slowly catching on.

"You can buy me a new bike for my birthday," laughed Sharon.

"CABBAGES!" they shouted.

And howled like wolves all the way down the Crescent.

AHHHH...